Daddy Is a Monster...
Sometimes

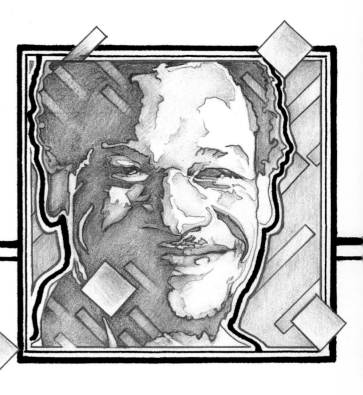

To
Dorothy Briley
Sheldon Fogelman
Janet Olsen
Christopher Poklewski
Ann White
Otis White

who knew more about getting through fear
than I, and who maintained confidence
in one who had almost lost it.

Especial thanks to Ron Irvis.

Daddy Is a Monster… Sometimes
Copyright © 1980 by John Steptoe
All rights reserved. Printed in the United States of America.

U.S. Library of Congress Cataloging in Publication Data
Steptoe, John, birth date
   Daddy is a monster… sometimes.

   SUMMARY: Bweela and Javaka relate the incidents
that make Daddy a monster in their eyes.
   [1. Fathers—Fiction]   I. Title.
PZ7.S8367Mu   [E]   77-4464
ISBN-0-397-31762-X
ISBN-0-397-31893-6 L.B.

10 9 8 7 6 5 4 3 2 1

First Edition

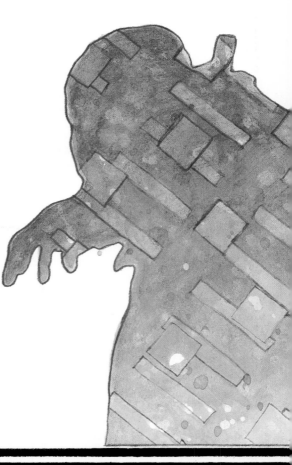

Daddy Is a Monster... Sometimes

JOHN STEPTOE

J. B. Lippincott
New York

We are Bweela and Javaka and we have a daddy. He's a nice daddy and all, but he got somethin' wrong with him. We was talkin' about him one day.

Javaka said, "Daddy gets like the monster in the scary movies, with teeth comin' out his mouth and hair all over his face."

"Yeah, Javaka, and his ears get pointy and he says, 'Grrraaw, go to bed! Grrraaw!' "

"That's right! Then he says, 'Grrraaw, go upstairs and play,' and then he gives you a spankin'. Right, Bweela?"

"Yeah, he's sure a mean old crazy monster… sometimes."

"Remember the time when we was at the ice cream store and Daddy bought us two ice cream cones?"

"And we was still eatin' them when we went grocery shopping. They was good. Wasn't they, Bweela?"

"Yeah, and then Daddy was lookin' at us eatin' them, and he said that he was gonna get him an ice cream cone after we finished shopping."

"But by the time we got back to the ice cream store, *our* ice cream was all gone. Daddy said to us, 'Now you might as well stick your lips back in, 'cause I already bought you guys ice cream, and one cone is enough for one day.'"

"And that's when it started to happen. That boogie monster! Hair started comin' out on his face, and—"

"But then this lady come in the store. She was nice to us. And she said, 'Oh, what cunning children! Aren't they having ice cream too?' "

"But Daddy said, 'Oh no, they just—' "

"Then she said, 'But it's such a hot afternoon and they're such darling children. Besides, I'm sure they'd enjoy ice cream as much as you're enjoying yours.' "

"And Daddy tried to stop her, but before he could tell her, the nice lady said to the store man, 'Yes, two large strawberry cones, please. Do you like strawberry, children?' "

" 'Yeah, we like it, lady,' we said."

"Then, Javaka, remember how Daddy was real angry and his teeth started growin' out like Dracula's? But when we got outside I tripped over a can and dropped my ice cream on the sidewalk. Daddy started to laugh at me, and I was so sad!"

"Yeah, Bweela, first he put his hand over his mouth. Then he didn't hold it back no more and he started laughin' out loud. 'Ha-ha-ha-ha.' Like that. I started eatin' my ice cream real quick before somethin' happened to it. That Daddy, he's a mean one all right!"

"Could I have some water, Dad?"

"Bweela, you know where the water faucet is. You can get it yourself."

"Daddy? How come you was laughin' at me when I dropped my ice cream at the store? That wasn't nice for you to do. I was sad at you."

"Bweela, it wasn't considerate of you to accept ice cream from that lady. I had already bought you a cone earlier, and you shouldn't have had your mouth stuck out like that when your poor old daddy was buying his."

"So.... But you didn't have to be doin' all that laughin', Daddy."

"Well, I knew it to be funny."

"Daddy?"

"What?"

"Where do the lights go when they go out?"

"Bweela, get out of my face, 'fore I knock you out."

"Daddy, you ain't gonna knock me out, 'cause I'm gonna give *you* a knuckle sandwich."

"Where's your brother at?"

"I don't know."

Sometimes Daddy is a monster in the nighttime. He be real nice and read you a story and everything, but then—when the story be over and he kiss you good-night and cut off the lights—he start to do it again. All you got to do is ask him for a little itsy-bitsy glass of water or say you got to go to the bathroom so you don't wet in the bed.... Then he start.

"Go to the bathroom!" he says. "Then go to sleep."

So then we both go to the bathroom and get back in bed. Then I say, "Daddy! Javaka won't give me my teddy bear!"

"It's not yours!" Javaka says.

"Daddy, Javaka got out of his bed! Daddy!"

Then when he's got enough of that he's a monster all over...and then he come up to the stairs and he be real mad.

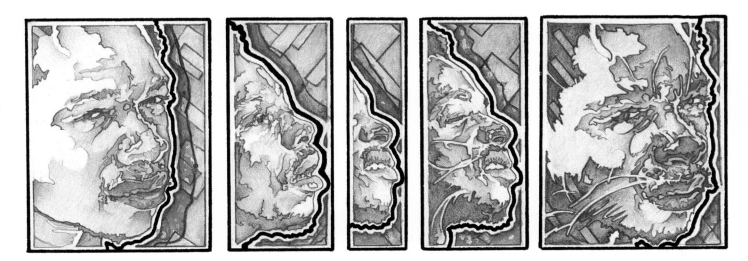

"If you don't be quiet I'm gonna shut the door to your room!" he says.

"But Daddy, we want another story," we say.

"Dad, I want some water. Daddy… Daddy, tell Javaka to stop singin'."

"Enough!" he says. Then he shuts the door and says, "That'll learn you, ha-ha-harrr!"

"Daddy, Daddy, we'll be quiet. We want the door open, just a little bit. Okay, please, Daddy?"

"All right, all right! But you'd better be good."

"Okay, Dad, we'll be good. Good-night Daddy."

"Daddy!"

"What!"

"We love you. See you in the mornin'."

When we go out to a restaurant Daddy sometimes turns into a monster, but only just a little bit so nobody sees him doin' it.

"If you don't stop playin' in your food and eat, I'm gonna take you into the bathroom and give you a spankin'," he'll say.

Sometimes Daddy's a monster when we want to

be a little messy....

…And sometimes he's a monster when we just want to make a little noise….

…And sometimes he turns into a monster when we have a little accident.

"Daddy, how come you turn into an ugly old monster sometimes?"

"What? Me—a monster? I'm never a monster."

"Yes, you are," we say. "Sometimes you a scary monster and you say, 'Go out and play. Grrraw.' And sometimes you say, 'Javaka, pick up all your toys. Grrraw!' "

"Oh, yeah. Well, I'm probably a monster daddy when I got monster kids."

"Daddy, you crazy," we say.

"Daddy is a monster, but only sometimes."
"Yeah, only sometimes."